Exploring Shapes™

Triangles

Bonnie Coulter Leech

The Rosen Publishing Group's
PowerKids Press™
New York

To Eve and Paulette, my two sisters—together we form a perfect triangle.

Published in 2007 by The Rosen Publishing Group, Inc.
29 East 21st Street, New York, NY 10010

First Edition

Editors: Daryl Heller and Kara Murray
Book Design: Elana Davidian

Photo Credits: Cover © Gavin Hellier/Getty Images; p. 5 © Sherman Hines/Masterfile; p. 7 © ArenaPal/Topham/The Image Works; p. 12 © Paul Eekhoff/Masterfile; p. 13 © George Hall/Corbis; p. 19 © Nicolas Sapieha/Corbis.

Library of Congress Cataloging-in-Publication Data

Leech, Bonnie Coulter.
  Triangles / Bonnie Coulter Leech.— 1st ed.
     p. cm. — (Exploring shapes)
  Includes bibliographical references and index.
  ISBN 1-4042-3495-0 (lib. bdg.)
  1. Triangle—Juvenile literature. 2. Shapes—Juvenile literature. I. Title. II. Series.
  QA482.L44 2007
  516'.154—dc22
                              2005030180

Manufactured in the United States of America

Contents

Things of Three

Have you ever noticed how many things around you come in threes? There are many stories with three characters. For example, there is the tale about the three little pigs. They built three houses to escape the big, bad wolf. In another tale Goldilocks visits the house of the three bears. Many children have also ridden tricycles, or bikes with three wheels. In the game of baseball it's three strikes and you're out!

In mathematics, or the study of numbers, there are some **geometric shapes** that have three sides and three angles. Geometric shapes with three sides and three angles are called triangles.

The sails on these sailboats form triangles. How many triangles do you see? Can you think of other objects that have the shape of triangles?

Polygons

Geometric shapes that have three or more sides are called polygons. Polygons are **closed** figures with three or more straight sides. If you trace the sides of a closed shape without lifting your finger, you will start and end at the same point. If the shape has an opening and you cannot trace it without picking up your finger, the shape is not closed.

Polygons are flat, two-dimensional shapes. Two-dimensional

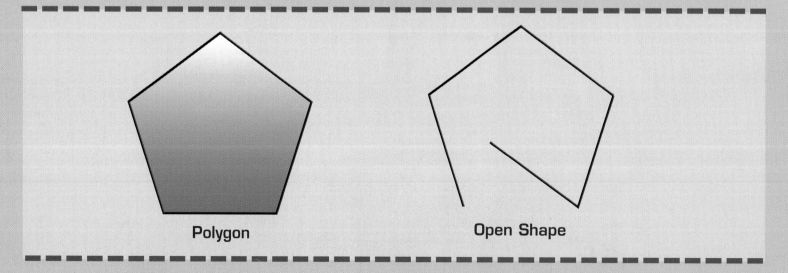

Polygon   **Open Shape**

shapes have only two **dimensions**, length and width. Two-dimensional shapes can be drawn on a flat surface, such as a flat sheet of paper.

The sides of a polygon are made of line segments. A line segment is part of a line with two endpoints. The endpoints, where the sides of a polygon meet, are called **vertices**.

Is this shape a polygon? If you look closely, you will see that two of the sides do not meet. Therefore, it is not a polygon.

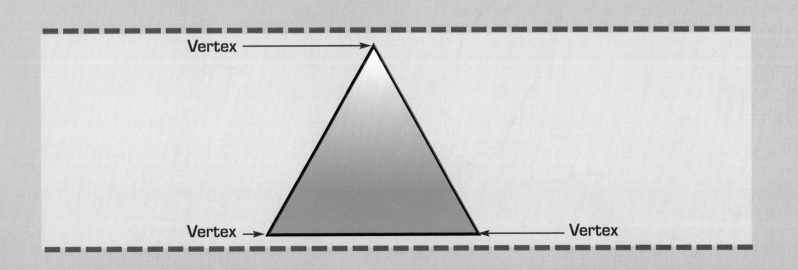

Vertex

Vertex

Vertex

Triangles

Polygons are given names based on the number of sides they have. The number of sides in a polygon will be equal to the number of vertices and the number of angles. This means that a polygon with five sides will also have five angles and five vertices.

A polygon with three sides and three angles is called a triangle. The word "tri" comes from the Greek word for "three." Therefore, the words "tri" and "angle" together mean "three angles."

The angles of a triangle are formed where the line segments that make up the sides meet at shared vertices. In some triangles the sides of a triangle are also called legs. Triangles are named using the three angles at the three vertices.

This is line segment AB.

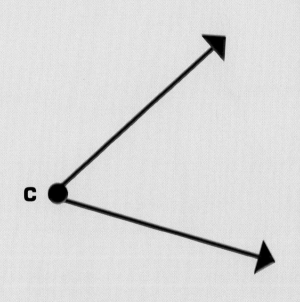

This is an angle with vertex C.
It is named angle C.

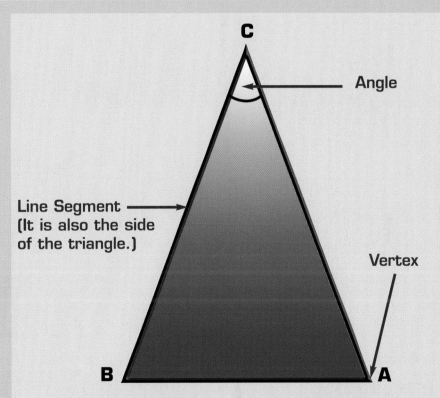

C

Angle

Line Segment
(It is also the side
of the triangle.)

Vertex

B   A

Triangles can be named using the letter
at each vertex. This is triangle ABC.

Parts of a Triangle

Let's take a closer look at a triangle. The vertex of a triangle is the point where two sides of a triangle meet to form an angle. At least two sides of a triangle are just called sides. The third side is sometimes called the base. The base is usually the side that the triangle sits on, or the lowest side. However, any one of the three sides could be the base.

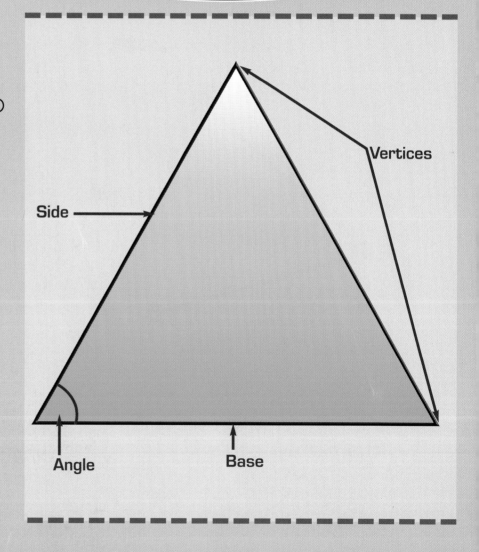

Vertices

Side

Angle

Base

The line segment that connects any vertex to the **midpoint** is called the median of the triangle. The midpoint is the middle of the side opposite the vertex.

The altitude is the **perpendicular** line segment drawn from one vertex to the opposite side.

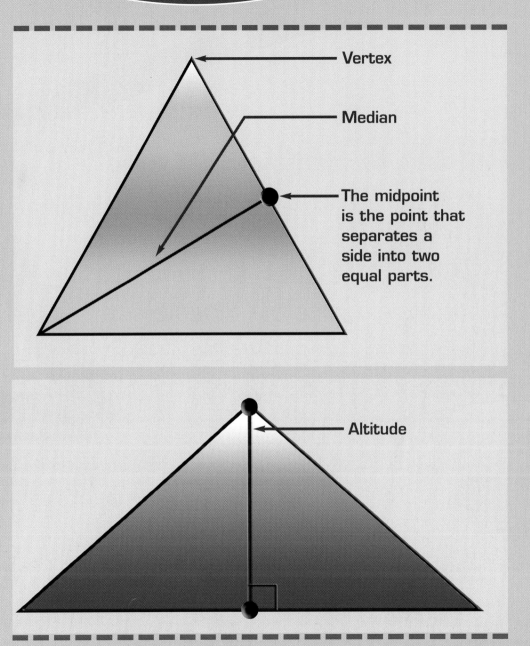

Vertex

Median

The midpoint is the point that separates a side into two equal parts.

Altitude

Naming Triangles

There are many ways to name a triangle. Since the vertices of a triangle are points, they are named with a single capital letter. Each triangle has three vertices. A triangle can be named using the letters for each of the three vertices.

To read the name of a triangle, look at the capital letter given for each vertex. Using the letter of each vertex, list the vertices in order going either **clockwise** or **counterclockwise**. This gives you many ways to name a triangle.

For example, the triangle on page 12 can be named △*ABC*, which is read triangle *ABC*. △ is the **symbol** for triangle. The same triangle can also be named △*ACB*, △*BAC*, △*BCA*, △*CAB*, and △*CBA*. Using this method there are six different ways to name this one triangle.

The wing of this fighter plane forms a triangle. To name this triangle, look at the capital letters at each vertex. How many ways can this triangle be named?

Triangles Classified by Sides

The sides of a triangle can be used to **classify** a triangle. If the measurements of two line segments are the same, we say the line segments are congruent. If the three sides of a triangle have the same measurement, the triangle is called an equilateral triangle. An equilateral triangle has three congruent, or equal, sides. If we break the word "equilateral" apart, "equi" means "equal" and "lateral" means "side."

A triangle that has two or more congruent sides is called an isosceles triangle. Isosceles means "two or more congruent sides." That means that an equilateral triangle, with three equal sides, is also an isosceles triangle.

A triangle can have no sides that have the same measurement. This triangle is called a scalene triangle.

Some sides of the triangles below have tick marks (/). Tick marks show which sides are congruent.

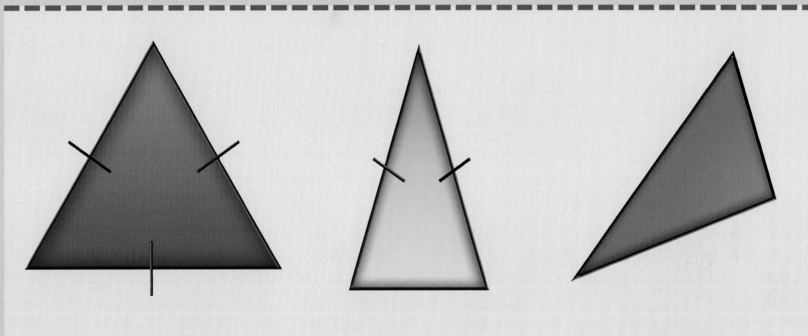

An equilateral triangle has all sides congruent.

An isosceles triangle has at least two sides congruent.

A scalene triangle has no sides that are congruent.

Triangles Classified by Angles

Angles can be used to classify triangles. Angles are measured in **degrees**. The symbol for degrees is °. The degree measure of an angle depends on how much it has been turned. No turn is 0° and one full turn is 360°.

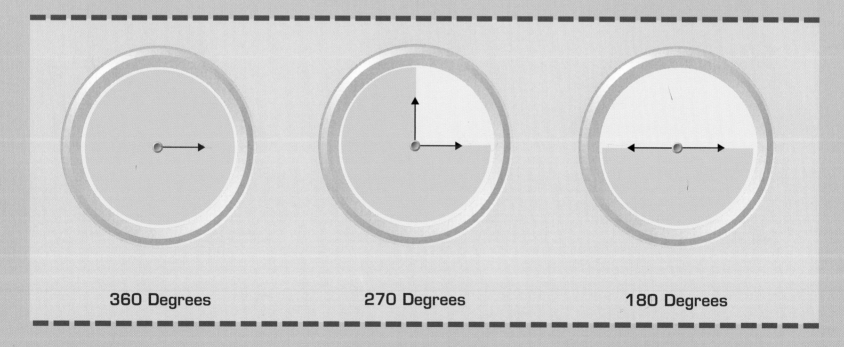

360 Degrees   270 Degrees   180 Degrees

Angles that measure greater than 0° but less than 90° are called acute angles. A triangle with three acute angles is called an acute triangle. Angles that measure greater than 90° but less than 180° are called obtuse angles. A triangle with one obtuse angle is called an obtuse triangle. Angles that measure 90° are called right angles. A triangle that has one 90° angle is called a right triangle.

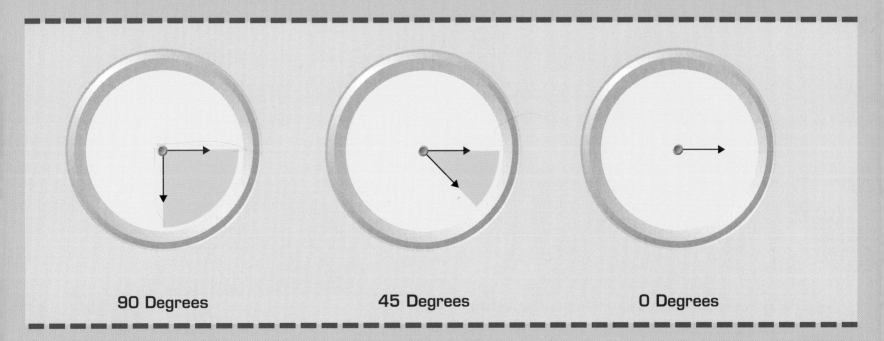

90 Degrees   45 Degrees   0 Degrees

In any triangle the sum of the measure of all three angles is 180°. A straight line segment also has a degree measure of 180°.

If you cut out the angles of a triangle and put them together, they will form a straight line segment. The two figures below show that when you add the three angles together, they will equal 180°.

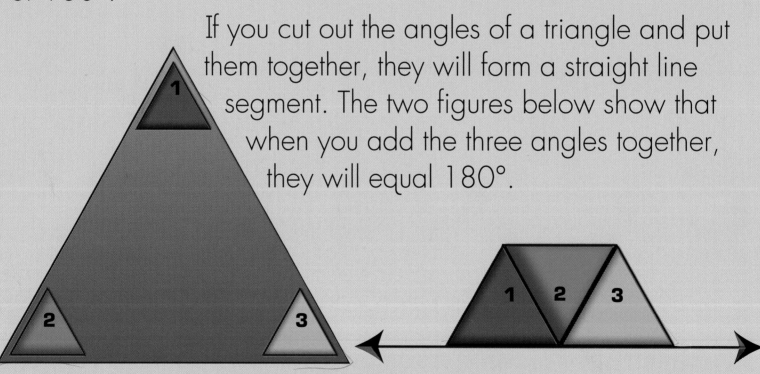

The sum of the measure of all the angles of a triangle equals 180°. Therefore, if a right angle measures 90°, the sum of the other two angles must be 90°. Those two angles are called acute, or angles that are less than 90°.

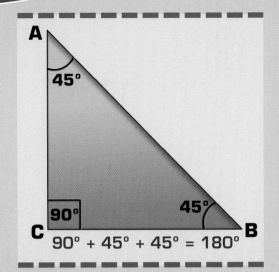

$$90° + 45° + 45° = 180°$$

Whether you find a triangle in a math book or on a wall, their angles will always add up to 180°!

The Perimeter and the Area of Triangles

Have you ever walked around a track? If so, then you walked the perimeter of that track. The perimeter of the track is the **distance** around the track.

The distance around the outside of any triangle is also called the perimeter. When you trace the outside of a triangle, you are tracing its perimeter. Start at one vertex and measure the distance to the next one. Do this for all three sides. If you are given the measurements for the lengths of the sides of a triangle, you can find the perimeter by adding the measurements of the sides.

The area of a geometric figure is the number of squares that it takes to cover its surface. The area of a triangle can be found by counting the number of squares that it takes to cover the inside of the triangle.

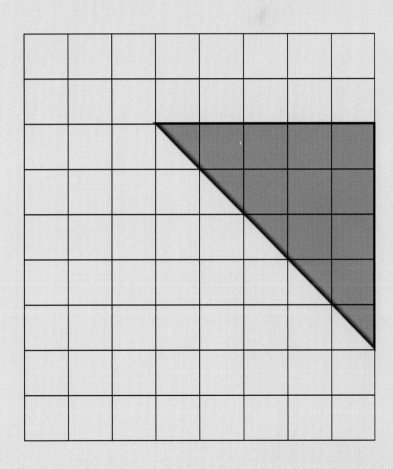

To find the area of this triangle, first count the whole squares. There are 10 whole squares. Then count the half squares. There are five half squares. Two half squares make one whole square, so five half squares make two and a half squares. 10 squares plus two and a half squares equal 12 and a half squares. The area of this triangle is 12 and a half squares.

Triangles Around Us

Triangles play an important part in the world around us. Triangles are two-dimensional geometric figures that have only the dimensions of length and width.

Three-dimensional shapes and objects have not only length and width but also height. Bridges are three-dimensional objects. Although a triangle is a two-dimensional figure, the shape of a triangle is often used in the building of bridges. A triangle is a shape that can hold much weight. Builders often use triangles to help make bridges stronger and sturdier.

Triangular shapes are also found in nature. If you look at a spiderweb, you will see many shapes inside the web that look like triangles.

Glossary

classify (KLA-seh-fy) To arrange in groups.

clockwise (KLOK-wyz) Moving in the direction that the hands of a clock move.

closed (KLOHZD) Having no openings.

counterclockwise (kown-ter-KLOK-wyz) Moving in the opposite direction that the hands of a clock move.

degrees (dih-GREEZ) Measurements of an angle or a part of a circle.

dimensions (duh-MEN-shunz) The length, width, or height of an object.

distance (DIS-tens) The length between two points.

geometric shapes (jee-uh-MEH-trik SHAYPS) Shapes in mathematics that may have points, lines, and surfaces, and that can be solid.

midpoint (MID-poynt) The middle point of a line segment.

perpendicular (per-pen-DIH-kyuh-ler) Having to do with two lines that cross to form four right, or 90º, angles.

symbol (SIM-bul) An object or a picture that stands for something else.

vertices (VER-tuh-seez) The points where two lines, line segments, or rays meet. Vertices are the plural, meaning more than one, of vertex.

Index

Web Sites

Due to the changing nature of Internet links, PowerKids Press has developed an online list of Web sites related to the subject of this book. This site is updated regularly. Please use this link to access the list:
www.powerkidslinks.com/psgs/triangles/